Twinkle

Flies High!

by Katharine Holabird • illustrated by Sarah Warburton

Ready-to-Read

Simon Spotlight
New York   London   Toronto   Sydney   New Delhi

SIMON SPOTLIGHT
An imprint of Simon & Schuster Children's Publishing Division
1230 Avenue of the Americas, New York, New York 10020
This Simon Spotlight edition December 2021
Text copyright © 2021 by Katharine Holabird
Illustrations copyright © 2021 by Sarah Warburton
Illustrations by Cherie Zamazing
For information about special discounts for bulk purchases,
please contact Simon & Schuster Special Sales at 1-866-506-1949 or
business@simonandschuster.com.
Manufactured in the United States of America 1021 LAK
10 9 8 7 6 5 4 3 2 1
Library of Congress Cataloging-in-Publication Data
Names: Holabird, Katharine, author. | Warburton, Sarah, illustrator.
Title: Twinkle flies high! / by Katharine Holabird ; illustrated by Sarah
Warburton.
Description: Simon Spotlight edition. | New York : Simon Spotlight, 2021. |
Series: Twinkle | Audience: Ages 5–7. | Summary: Twinkle wants to win first
place in the Fairy Fly Race, so she practices every day with her friends.
Identifiers: LCCN 2021025625 (print) | LCCN 2021025626 (ebook) |
ISBN 9781534496743 (hardcover) | ISBN 9781534496736 (paperback) |
ISBN 9781534496750 (ebook)
Subjects: CYAC: Fairies—Fiction. | Racing—Fiction. | Friendship—Fiction. |
LCGFT: Picture books.
Classification: LCC PZ7.H689 Twjw 2021 (print) | LCC PZ7.H689 (ebook) |
DDC [E]—dc23
LC record available at https://lccn.loc.gov/2021025625
LC ebook record available at https://lccn.loc.gov/2021025626

"Calling all fairies!"
Miss Flutterbee said.
"It is almost time for
Fairy Field Day at
The Fairy School of Magic
and Music!"

"There will be fun
and races for everyone,"
said Miss Flutterbee.
"The winner of each race
will get rainbow cupcakes
with rainbow sprinkles."

Twinkle's classmate Buttercup
was really excited.
"I love racing almost as much
as I love rainbow sprinkles!"
Buttercup said.

Twinkle and her friends
Lulu and Pippa were excited too.
"I would love to win the
Fairy Fly Race," said Twinkle.

"I want to try the
Flower Hop race," said Pippa.
"We will all have to practice hard,"
Lulu said.

Twinkle practiced flying every day after school with her friends in the Sparkle Tree Forest.

First, she raced with Dr. Hoooo,
the wise old owl.
"Ready, set, fly!" said Dr. Hoooo.
Twinkle could barely keep up.
Owls fly very fast!

"You won!" said Twinkle.
"Whoooo, me?" said Dr. Hoooo.
"Maybe you will win next time."

They raced again.
Twinkle did not win,
but she did fly faster!

The next day, Twinkle practiced flying
with her pet dragon, Scruffy.
They flew side by side . . .
and Scruffy showed Twinkle
how to do loop-the-loops in the air.
"I love flying loop-the-loops!"
Twinkle said.

Scruffy was in the lead
until he spotted blueberries below
and stopped for a snack.
"Oh, Scruffy!" Twinkle said
and flew down to join him.

Next, Twinkle raced
with Boris the bat.
Boris flew up, down,
and all around at top speed,
and Twinkle tried her best
to follow him.

"That was a lot of work!"
Twinkle said.
Boris flapped his wings and winked.
Twinkle used her magic
to make a hammock for a nap!

The next day, Tweeter the bluebird
showed Twinkle how to soar
high in the sky.
"Everything looks so tiny
and pretty from up here,"
Twinkle said.

Twinkle was flying faster than ever.
"I think I am ready for
the Fairy Fly Race!"
she told Tweeter.

Soon it was Fairy Field Day.
Twinkle had practiced a lot,
but she was so nervous
that her wings glowed green.

Miss Flutterbee said,
"Good morning, fairies!
Please use your fairy magic to
make a special outfit for your race.
Then we will get started."

The sound of excited fairies
fluttering their wings and
whispering magic spells filled the air.
Twinkle raised her wand
and made her own special spell.

"Fairies and rainbows,
and sparkly wings, please.
Dress me so I can fly as fast
as a breeze!" she shouted.

Poof!
Twinkle looked down in surprise.
She was dressed up just like
a fluffy, puffy cloud!

Twinkle liked her cloud,
but then she saw the other fairies
all wearing outfits
with racing stripes.

Buttercup smiled and said,
"I love your special outfit, Twinkle.
Good luck today!"

"Oh, thank you!" said Twinkle.
"Good luck, too, Buttercup!"

It was time for the
Flower Hop race to begin.
The fairies had to hop over
a field of flowers and skip
to the finish line.
Lulu and Pippa were both
in the race.

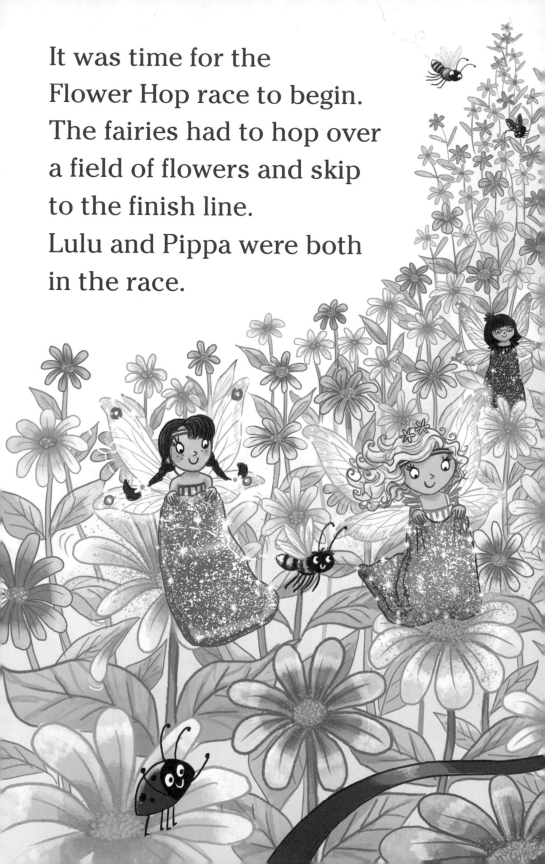

Miss Flutterbee rang a bell,
and the race began!
Lulu giggled as she hopped
over each flower.
But Pippa was determined.
She hopped and skipped so quickly
that she raced by all the other fairies.
Pippa won!

Twinkle cheered for Pippa.
Then she started to feel
nervous again.
The Fairy Fly Race was
about to start!
As Twinkle joined the other
fairies at the starting line,
Miss Flutterbee flew over to her.

"Are you feeling okay?"
Miss Flutterbee asked.
Twinkle shook her head.
"I am feeling nervous," she said.
"Just do the best you can do,
and try to have fun,"
said Miss Flutterbee kindly.

The bell rang, and the race began!
Twinkle soared up high
and flapped her wings
as hard as she could.
She remembered all she had learned
from her Sparkle Tree Forest
friends.

Even so, Twinkle was not fast enough.
Buttercup won the race.
"Fairytastic, Buttercup!" Twinkle said.
"Thank you, Twinkle," Buttercup said.

"Sorry you did not win,"
said Pippa to Twinkle.
"It is okay," said Twinkle.
"I will try again next time.
I may not have been the fastest
fairy today, but I flew faster
than I ever have,
and I had a lot of fun!"

Miss Flutterbee rang the bell again and said she had a new prize to give. "This prize is for the most original outfit, and it goes to . . . Twinkle!" Twinkle was so happy, her wings glowed in rainbow colors!

Buttercup and Pippa and Twinkle shared their prizes with all the fairies. It was a magical Fairy Field Day!